Happy Pet Friends

RABBITS

Written by Izzi Howell
Illustrated by Charlotte Cotterill

WAYLAND

First published in Great Britain in 2022 by Wayland

Produced for Wayland by
White-Thomson Publishing Ltd
www.wtpub.co.uk

HB ISBN: 978 1 5263 1685 1
PB ISBN: 978 1 5263 1686 8

Credits
Author and editor: Izzi Howell
Illustrator: Charlotte Cotterill
Designer: Clare Nicholas
Cover designer: Ellie Boultwood
Proofreader: Annabel Stones

The publisher would like to thank the following for permission to reproduce their photographs:
Alamy: Juniors Bildarchiv GmbH 6t and 19; Getty: pets-in-frames 4br, Daniil Dubov 9c, Jon Lauriat 10, Bobex-73 12, Evelien Doosje 14c, IRYNA KAZLOVA 17t and 29r, Patrick Daxenbichler 20t, Boogich 21, Nadeika 24c, kali9 26; Shutterstock: Djem cover and title page, JIANG HONGYAN 2, 6b, 22t and 24t, Oleksandr Lytvynenko 4tl, 8c, 17b and 31, Tsekhmister 4tr, slowmotiongli 4bl, Eric Isselee, Dorottya Mathe and Medvedev Andrey 5b, goodbishop 7, Andrii Medvediuk 8t, Photobac 8b, Garna Zarina 9t, kurhan 9b, Samuel Borges Photography 11 and 28, STEKLO 13, Nattaro Ohe 14t, 23t and 29l, Quinn Martin 14b, Dollydoll29 15 and 22b, anetapics 16, cynoclub 18 and 25, rob3rt82 20b, Sven Boettcher 23b, Artsiom P 24b, Roselynne 27.
All design elements from Shutterstock.

Printed and bound in China

Wayland, an imprint of
Hachette Children's Group
Part of Hodder and Stoughton
Carmelite House
50 Victoria Embankment
London EC4Y 0DZ

An Hachette UK Company
www.hachettechildrens.co.uk

Contents

The Perfect Pet

Rabbits can make perfect pets! They are friendly, fun and very clever. But bringing home bunnies is a **BIG** responsibility. They can live for 8 to 12 years, so you will need to take care of them for a long time. Rabbits are **SOCIAL** animals, so you'll need to adopt at least **TWO** rabbits for them to live 'hoppily' ever after!

A rabbit's ***fluffy tail*** is coloured on top and white underneath.

Their ***long back legs*** help them to hop along.

THERE ARE MANY DIFFERENT BREEDS OF RABBIT.

Their ears and fur can be long or short. Some are tiny and some are huge! You can keep different breeds of rabbits together.

The **Blanc de Hotot rabbit** looks like it's wearing sunglasses!

This isn't a baby bunny – it's a **dwarf rabbit**! This type of rabbit is much smaller than other breeds.

Big eyes on the sides of their head mean that they can see nearly all the way around them.

Rabbits have ***long ears*** that they can move in lots of directions.

A happy bunny wriggles its ***nose*** non-stop!

Rabbits use their ***strong front paws*** to dig.

Furry Friend FACT!

Flemish Giants are the biggest bunny breed. The longest rabbit ever was a Flemish Giant who was 129 centimetres long. That's as long as a medium-sized dog!

Lop-eared rabbits have long, floppy ears.

The stylish **lionhead rabbit** gets its name from the fluffy mane around its head!

Angora rabbits are the fluffiest rabbits. What a fuzzball!

Rex rabbits have short, velvety fur.

Home Sweet Home

Most breeds of rabbit can live indoors or outdoors, as long as they have lots of space to **PLAY** and **HOP** around. A pair of average-sized rabbits needs an enclosure that is at least 3 metres long, 2 metres wide and 1 metre high.

These rabbits have everything they need in their enclosure, plus lots of toys for fun!

COSY CARE

To help your rabbits stay healthy, they need:

Soft bedding to snuggle in, such as hay or shredded paper

Furry Friend FACT!

Rabbits can jump up to 90 centimetres in one hop! So they need plenty of height in their enclosure, and tall sides so that they can't hop out!

Whether your rabbits live **INDOORS** or **OUTDOORS**, they need a special shelter in their enclosure to hide away and **SNOOZE** in. They should be able to move in and out of their shelter whenever they want.

The bedding in your rabbits' shelter needs to be changed every week.

A **safe shelter** in a **large enclosure**

Fresh food and **water** every day

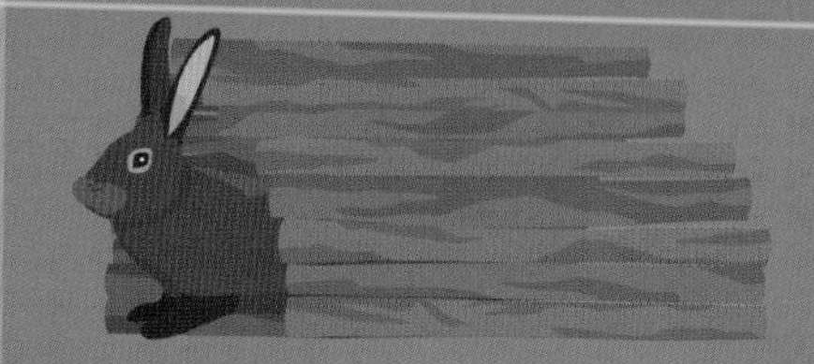

Fun toys to play with.

Favourite Food

The right diet will help to keep your rabbits healthy. Eating the right food is especially **IMPORTANT** for your rabbits' **TEETH**.

WHAT YOUR RABBITS NEED EVERY DAY:

Fresh drinking **WATER** that is always available – you should check it twice a day.

Some rabbits like to drink water from a bowl, while others use a water bottle.

Good quality **HAY** or fresh **GRASS** – this is your rabbits' main food.

Each rabbit needs a bundle of hay the same size as them to eat every day!

Some **LEAFY GREEN PLANTS**, such as cabbage, broccoli or mint.

Introduce new greens bit by bit so that your bunnies don't get an upset tummy!

A small amount of rabbit **PELLETS** – give each rabbit 25 grams of pellets for each kilogram of its body weight.

Rabbit pellets contain vitamins and minerals that your bunnies need to stay fit and strong!

Furry Friend FACT!

Rabbits should eat carrots rarely and as a treat! Rabbits don't naturally eat root vegetables or fruit, so eating too much can make them ill.

Special rabbit mueslis are often sold in pet shops, but they aren't very good for your rabbits' **HEALTH**. If you already feed your rabbits muesli, talk to your **VET** about changing over to a healthier **DIET**.

Rabbits love to munch on **GRASS**, but don't feed them grass cuttings from a lawnmower as this can give them an **UPSET STOMACH!** This is because grass cut by a lawnmower ferments very quickly.

Handle with Care

As well as hanging out with other bunnies, rabbits also need lots of love and attention from their owners. But **HANDLING** them in the wrong way makes them very 'un-hoppy'! Speak **QUIETLY**, move **SLOWLY** and touch them **GENTLY** to keep your rabbits relaxed.

Baby rabbits are called kittens! It's important to handle rabbits from a young age so that they get used to it.

CALL THAT A PURR?!

Furry Friend FACT!

Rabbits purr when they are happy! A rabbit purr sounds like a quiet clicking noise. They make the sound by rubbing their teeth together.

When you **PICK UP** a rabbit, use one hand to **SUPPORT** their back legs and back. Holding all four of their feet against your body or holding them on your lap will help them to feel safe. **NEVER** hold them upside down as this makes them feel **SCARED**.

Hold your rabbit close to the floor in case they make a hop for freedom!

Gentle Grooming

Taking care of your rabbits' nails and fur will keep them **HEALTHY** and **HAPPY**! Moving around and being active is often enough to keep your rabbits' nails from getting too long. Their nails should be the same length as the fur on their toes.

If your rabbits' nails are too long, they will need to be snipped with special clippers. This should be done by a vet or an adult.

Rabbits **GROOM** themselves, but they also need a helping hand from their owners. If not, they can swallow a lot of **FUR**, which makes them sick. You should groom your rabbits **EVERY DAY**.

This funny-looking glove is a bunny grooming mitt! You can also use a special grooming comb or brush.

Furry Friend FACT!

The longest fur recorded on a rabbit was 36.5 centimetres long!

Gnawing Gnashers

Rabbits' teeth never stop growing! However, the hay and grass that your rabbits eat **WEAR DOWN** their teeth, so they shouldn't get too long.

Hay and grass keep rabbits' teeth and tummies healthy!

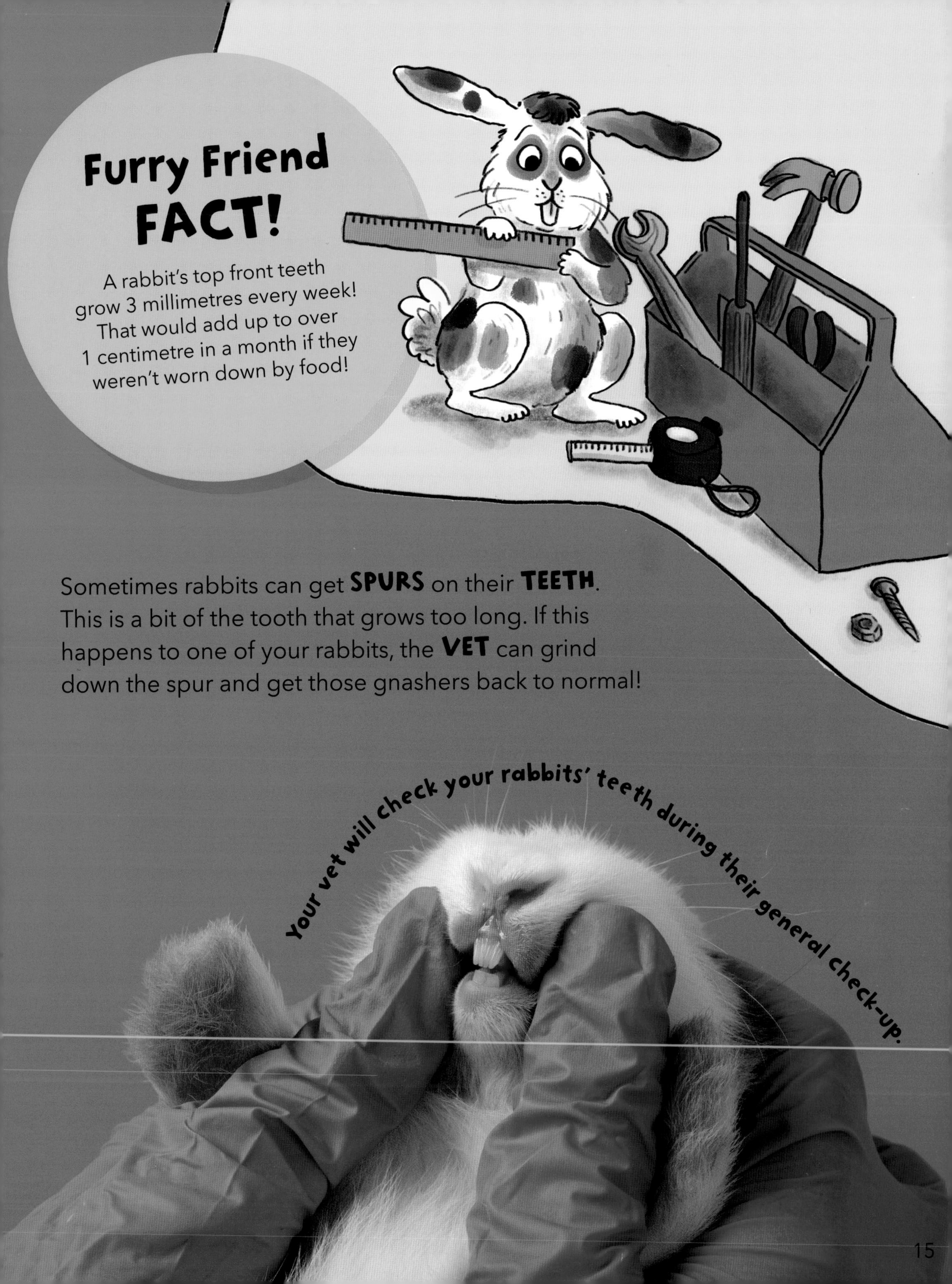

Sometimes rabbits can get **SPURS** on their **TEETH**. This is a bit of the tooth that grows too long. If this happens to one of your rabbits, the **VET** can grind down the spur and get those gnashers back to normal!

Busy Body, Happy Bunny

Rabbits are playful animals. They need **ENTERTAINMENT** or they will become **BORED** bunnies! One of the best rabbit toys is a **PLATFORM** to hop on and off. The platform could be a wooden crate, a straw bale or a tree stump.

If your rabbits love jumping, check with your vet if you can try doing rabbit agility courses with them! This is good entertainment for some rabbits.

Rabbits love to **DIG**, so why not give them a **PIT** of child-friendly **SAND** or earth to play with! Your bunnies will also enjoy crawling through **TUNNELS** and playing with **CARDBOARD BOXES**.

Pet rabbits get their digging skills from their wild cousins, who dig burrows to live in.

Boo! Rabbits love hiding in cardboard boxes.

Furry Friend FACT!

Rabbits are crepuscular, which means they are most active around sunrise and sunset! So you may find your bunnies having fun when you're just waking up!

Train Your Brainy Bunny

Rabbits are very clever and can be taught some **SIMPLE TRICKS**, such as coming when called. **TRAINING** keeps your bunnies busy and entertained, which makes them **HAPPY**!

Why not train your rabbits to run through a fabric tunnel? It's fun and good exercise!

INDOOR RABBITS can be trained to use a **LITTER TRAY**. Having a special toilet zone makes it much easier to keep things clean. Make sure you **CLEAN** their litter tray every day to stop it from getting **STINKY**!

Fill your rabbits' litter tray with hay, newspaper or special litter.

Furry Friend FACT!

All you need to train your rabbits is a clicker and a healthy food treat. Click and give a treat every time the rabbits do the right action. Your bunnies will quickly learn that doing the action means a reward!

Safety First

Whether your rabbits live indoors or outdoors, you must make sure their environment is SAFE. Outdoor rabbits need **SHADE** on sunny days. They must be **PROTECTED** from the wind and rain.

An outdoor enclosure keeps rabbits safe from other animals and poisonous plants.

All houseplants and many garden plants, such as daffodils, ivy and bluebells, are **POISONOUS** to rabbits.

If your rabbits live **INDOORS**, you need to **BUNNY-PROOF** your house! Keep your rabbits far away from other pets, and any wires or cables that they could nibble on. Walk around **CAREFULLY** so that you don't accidentally stand on them!

Furry Friend FACT!

An old legend states that rabbits once sank a ship by chewing a hole in the side! Today, some sailors still think it's bad luck to bring a rabbit on a boat!

Bunny Behaviour

Your bunnies can talk to you with their bodies! If your rabbit rubs its nose on you, it might want you to move or pay it more **ATTENTION**. When both of its ears are up, it means that it is **CURIOUS** about its surroundings.

SORRY ...
WHAT?

One ear up and one ear down means that your rabbit is listening but not totally paying attention.

Furry Friend FACT!

Rabbits can turn their ears 180 degrees so they can listen to everything going on around them!

The **BINKY** is the ultimate sign of a **HAPPY** bunny! It is a jump with a twist of the legs or body in the air. A binky is a sign that your rabbit feels **EXCITED** or **PLAYFUL**.

Watch your bunnies closely to learn their favourite things that make them want to do a binky!

Are My Rabbits Ill?

It's important to get to know your rabbits and their normal habits so you can tell if something is wrong. Look out for any **CHANGES** in **BEHAVIOUR**, **EATING**, going to the **TOILET** or **SLEEPING**.

ZZZZ!

It's normal for rabbits to hide sometimes, but if a bunny never comes out of its hiding place, it might be stressed.

Check over your bunnies' bodies every day. **GROOMING** is often a good time to do this! Look at their fur, eyes, nose, ears and teeth. If you are **WORRIED** about anything, it's time for your rabbits to visit the **VET**!

Your rabbit's fur should be smooth and clean with no bald bits.

Furry Friend FACT!

Rabbits need to eat their own poo to stay healthy! The first soft poo they produce is full of nutrients, so they eat it again! When it comes out for the second time, the poo is hard and dry.

A Trip to the Vet

Your rabbits need a check-up at the VET once a year. You will also need to take your rabbits in for **VACCINATIONS** when they are young. Take a rabbit to the vet immediately if it looks like they are in pain or if they might have eaten something poisonous.

Your vet will check every part of your rabbits during their check-up.

It is best to get your rabbits **NEUTERED** or **SPAYED** at the vets so that they can't have babies. This will help them get on better with other bunnies. You also won't have any **SURPRISE** bunny babies!

Rabbits have around six kittens per litter, but they can get pregnant again very soon afterwards. If you aren't careful, you can end up with a bunch of bunnies!

Furry Friend FACT!

The most rabbit kittens ever recorded in one litter was 24!

Pet Pop Quiz

Test your rabbit knowledge with this pop quiz! The more you know about your pet, the happier and healthier it will be in your care.

HOW MANY DID YOU GET RIGHT?

Answers:

1. 8 to 12 years; **2.** Hay or fresh grass; **3.** Only occasionally as a treat; **4.** As long as the fur on their toes; **5.** In case they jump off your lap; **6.** Every day; **7.** A pit of child-friendly sand or earth; **8.** It keeps them away from poisonous plants and other animals; **9.** A jump with a twist of the body or legs in the air that shows that your rabbits feel happy; **10.** So that they get on better with other rabbits and don't have any surprise babies.

Glossary

binky a special jump with a twist of the body or legs that shows that your rabbit is happy

breed a type of animal or plant

burrow a hole that a wild rabbit digs to live in

enclosure an area surrounded by fences

ferment to go through a chemical change and turn into alcohol

gnawing nibble on something continuously to wear it away

groom to clean an animal's fur

litter all of the babies that an animal has at one time

neuter to stop an animal from being able to have babies

nutrient a substance that an animal needs to be healthy

poisonous something that can cause damage if eaten

responsibility to be dependable, make good choices and take account of your actions, often for the good of something else

spay to stop a female animal from being able to have babies

vaccination a type of medicine that stops you or an animal from getting a disease

vet someone who gives animals medical care and treatment

BOOKS TO READ

My New Pet: Rabbit by Jinny Johnson (Franklin Watts, 2013)

Pet Expert: Rabbits by Gemma Barder (Wayland, 2020)

Pet Pals: Rabbits by Pat Jacobs (Wayland, 2018)

FURTHER INFORMATION

To find out more about rabbits and how you can look after your pet to keep it happy and healthy, you can visit these websites:

www.rspca.org.uk/adviceandwelfare/pets/rabbits
Find lots of information about your rabbit's living space, diet and behaviour.

rabbitwelfare.co.uk/rabbit-care-advice/ownership/think-you-want-a-rabbit/
Learn more about what you need to consider before becoming a rabbit owner.

www.bluecross.org.uk/pet-advice/rabbit-facts
Discover some more fun rabbit facts!

Index

Titles in the **Happy Pet Friends** series!

GUINEA PIGS

The Perfect Pet
Home Sweet Home
Favourite Food
Gnawing Gnashers
Handle with Care
Gentle Grooming
Busy Bodies
It's Good to Talk
Safety First!
Brilliant Body Clues
Is My Guinea Pig Ill?
A Trip to the Vet
Pet Pop Quiz

CATS

The Perfect Pet
Home Comforts
Best of Friends
Cat Cuddles
Feeding Time!
Play Time!
Body Language
Stress Busters
Cat Chat
Call of the Wild
Scaredy Cats
A Trip to the Vet
Pet Pop Quiz

DOGS

The Perfect Pet
Home Sweet Home
Creature Comforts
Feeding Time!
Out and About
Lessons for Life
Best Friends
Let's Get Moving!
Barks, Growls, Woofs and Howls
Sighs, Groans, Yawns and Moans
Body Talk
A Trip to the Vet
Pet Pop Quiz

RABBITS

The Perfect Pet
Home Sweet Home
Favourite Food
Handle with Care
Gentle Grooming
Gnawing Gnashers
Busy Body, Happy Bunny
Train your Brainy Bunny
Safety First
Bunny Behaviour
Are My Rabbits Ill?
A Trip to the Vet
Pet Pop Quiz

HAMSTERS

The Perfect Pet
Dwarf Hamster Duos
Home Sweet Home
Peace and Quiet
Nourishing Nibbles
Handle with Care
Gnawing Gnashers
Keeping Clean
Happy Hamster Toys
Safety First
Is My Hamster Ill?
A Trip to the Vet
Pet Pop Quiz

FISH

Great Goldfish
Feeling Tropical
Fishy Friends
Tank Sweet Tank
Bright and Warm
Aquarium Additions
Wonderful Water
Keeping Clean
Fishy Dishes
Feeling Fin-tastic
Some Fin Wrong?
Babies and Bubbles
Pet Pop Quiz